BLAIRSVILLE SENIOR HIGH SCHOOL
BLAIRSVILLE, PENNA.

Rookie Summer

Bill Gutman
AR B.L.: 3.5
Points: 2.0

Rookie Summer

By
Bill Gutman

Turman Publishing,
a division of Educational Design, Inc., New York

Author: Bill Gutman
Cover Illustration: Kevin Mayes
Cover Design: Linda Turman
Series Editor: Louise Morgan
Copy Editor: Deborah Annan

ISBN# 0-89872-300-0   EDI E300

For Cathy

Rookie Summer

1

Barney Rogers took a deep breath as he sat down on the old, rotting, wooden bleachers at Wilson Park. What a day to have your car break down, he thought to himself. And in a place like Caldwell, Iowa, no less.

But such was the life of a big league baseball scout. You drove the back roads of Nowheresville, U.S.A., looking for ballplayers. And you never knew where you'd find them. So when Barney heard there was a men's league game in progress, he felt that the day wasn't a total loss.

"At least it's baseball," he said softly to himself as he watched the strange collection of middle age and younger men on the roughed-out diamond. The infield had tufts of grass growing here and there, and the outfield sloped and rolled, looking more like a dirt bike course than a place to play ball.

Barney watched almost droopy-eyed for about five minutes. But that was before he noticed the kid. He was playing centerfield for one of the teams, the Rockets, and was obviously much younger than the other players. Barney could spot in a minute that there was something special about him.

The youngster was just a shade under six feet tall, weighed maybe 190 pounds, and looked very solid. Even though the boy had more of an athlete's body than any of the men out there, Barney could tell he was very young.

The old scout sat upright on the bleachers and began studying the kid. Barney noticed how he changed position with each batter. And how he began to move with each pitch. Things you can't really teach. Just then there was a long fly hit into the right centerfield gap.

Sure enough, the kid was running with the crack of the bat. Barney watched the ease with which he ran the ball down. He used his outstanding speed to get there, then slowed down just enough to catch the ball by his left shoulder. Like all the great ones, he had made a tough catch look easy.

As the teams changed sides, Barney walked over to a young boy who was watching the game. He tapped the youngster on the shoulder.

"You know who that is?" Barney asked, pointing toward the young ballplayer sitting by himself at the end of the bench.

"Who?" the young boy asked.

"That kid at the end of the bench."

"Oh, him. That's Bobby Blaine. He's the best darned baseball player around," the boy said.

"Around where?"

"Anywhere. I know he's the best player I've

ever seen. As good as some of those guys on television.''

''How old is he?'' Barney asked, again eying the youngster and now anxious to see him hit.

''I dunno. Maybe 16. Think he's got two more years of high school.''

''Thanks,'' Barney said, slipping the youngster a dollar. ''Buy yourself a soda or something.''

''Gee, thanks mister,'' the boy said.

Barney made some quick notes on a pad he always carried with him. Then he settled back to watch the game. It wasn't until the next inning that Bobby Blaine finally came to bat. There were runners on first and second, two out. The pitcher was a burly right-hander with a pretty good fastball but spotty control.

The youngster was a right-handed batter who stood with a slightly closed stance in the middle of the batter's box. He looked relaxed, but Barney could see the muscles in his forearms as he wigwagged the bat at the pitcher.

Bobby took the first pitch for a strike. The next was high and tight. The youngster pulled his head back calmly as the ball sailed past his chin. Barney continued to make notes on the pad.

The third pitch was belt high, slightly outside. Bobby stepped into it and took a powerful cut. The line drive flew into the right centerfield gap and rolled between the outfielders. Barney watched the speed with which the youngster circled the bases. He cut each bag just right and slid head-first into third in a way that would have made Rickey Henderson proud.

Two innings later, Barney watched as Bobby Blaine made a powerful throw from center to nail a runner at home. The ball came in like a bullet on the fly and didn't get more than five feet off the ground. The old scout couldn't believe what he was seeing. He forgot where he was for an instant and spoke out loud.

"This kid has it all," he said.

2

Barney Rogers watched the rest of the game in wonder. He had never seen a kid this young who was this good. Bobby got two more hits, including a long home run. The only time they got him out was when he hit a line drive right at the third baseman.

He also made a couple of other great plays in the outfield and seemed to enjoy every minute of the ballgame. The old scout wasn't sure whether he should talk to the young player or not. The problem was solved when the game ended. Before Barney could climb down from the bleachers, Bobby jumped into a car with two other boys and was gone.

Not one to leave anything to chance, Barney made some phone calls. He spoke with Paul Tuttle, coach of the Caldwell High School baseball team. Bobby Blaine, indeed, would be entering his junior year. He was barely 16 years old, but had been a star baseball player since he hit three home runs in his very first Little League game.

Tuttle said all that Bobby wanted was to be a big league ballplayer. In fact, that was all he ever wanted. Barney told Tuttle he'd be back but made the coach promise not to mention anything to Bobby, just in case.

————

Barney Rogers left town the next afternoon when the repairs were finished on his car. As he drove down Main Street on his way to the highway, he passed Boswell's Drug Store, where three boys sat inside, sipping sodas.

"Maybe this will be the year a scout shows up," Bobby Blaine was saying to Josh Martin, his best friend, and another boy, Steve Ferris. "All I want is for someone to see me play."

"Do you really think big league scouts are going to come to a tiny hick town in the middle of Iowa?" Steve asked.

"Why shouldn't they?" Josh asked quickly. He was not only Bobby's best friend, but his biggest fan as well. "Heck, maybe I'll write to some big league teams myself."

Steve laughed. "That's a good one. I *know* they wouldn't listen to you."

"Hey, it's not impossible," Bobby said. "Aren't scouts supposed to go everywhere looking for ballplayers?"

"But Caldwell?" Steve asked again.

"I just want some kind of shot," Bobby said. "Maybe if someone sees me play, I'll get a contract and a chance to start out in the minors."

"If that happened, would you really go?" Steve asked, as if he were just beginning to understand what Bobby was saying. "You'd really leave here, leave your family and friends?"

"Wouldn't you if you had the chance to play in the big leagues?" asked Josh. "Can't you imagine yourself playing with the greatest ballplayers in the world and making a million bucks at the same time?"

Steve looked at the ceiling, as if he were trying to picture himself playing with the New York Yankees or the Kansas City Royals. Josh was grinning, while Bobby was making a hissing sound with his straw at the bottom of his glass.

"Nope," Steve finally said. "I can't imagine myself doing that."

Josh laughed and shook his head. "I don't know about you, Ferris. Why do you make everything so tough?"

"Cuz he can't hit a curveball," Bobby said. "I'd like to have a dollar for every time I struck him out since Little League."

"You'd be rich," Josh quipped.

"Rich, maybe," said Steve. "But striking me out won't get you to the big leagues."

"Of course not, nerd," said Josh, once again defending his friend. "Bobby's going as a center-fielder, not as a pitcher."

"Hey, if he's not gonna pitch, maybe I can go, too," Steve said. "Because there won't be anyone to strike me out."

"My grandmother could strike you out," said Josh. "Come to think of it, so could I."

"And you're almost as good as your grandmother," Steve shot back.

"Leave my grandmother out of it," Josh said, winking at Bobby. "She's starting to lose her curveball."

"And you never had one."

"Hey, Bobby," Josh said. "Old Ferris wheel is really sharp today. He ought to buy us a soda since we have to listen to his wit."

"You got a point there," said Bobby.

"Tell you what," Steve said. "I *am* gonna buy you guys a soda, and then we're all gonna toast Bobby, cuz I do think he's gonna make it to the big leagues."

"You and I finally agree on something," said Josh.

As Steve went to the counter for the sodas, Bobby couldn't help wondering. Was he really good enough to make it? Maybe playing against guys like Steve Ferris or being in the men's league wasn't a real test. Maybe striking out Steve or hitting a home run against Benny Wilson, as he had done yesterday, didn't mean a thing. Maybe they just weren't that good. Maybe he just wasn't that good. But if that was really the way it was, Bobby hoped he would find out soon.

3

As a junior, Bobby Blaine was almost a one-man team for Caldwell High. He pitched, played centerfield, and even saw some action at shortstop. In addition, he was the fastest runner on the team and could hit anything. There wasn't a pitcher in the Tri-County League who could stop him.

But as good as Bobby was, there was one thing bothering him. Would there ever be a big league scout watching him? He asked Coach Tuttle about this several times, but the conversation was almost always the same.

"We're kind of off the beaten path here, Bobby," the coach said. "And we've never had a player from Caldwell sign a professional contract. So I guess we're not really considered a hotbed of talent. Besides, scouts sometimes wait until a kid is a senior before talking to him. But you never know who's watching."

The coach was thinking about Barney Rogers. He didn't want to break the promise he had made to him, or get Bobby's hopes up in case the scout didn't bother to return.

"You know how I feel about the game," Bobby

said. "How will I have a chance if no one sees me play?"

"Tell you what," the coach said. "If no one comes here this year, then I'll write to every big league team about you before next season begins."

"You got a deal, Coach. And I'll make sure you have plenty to write about."

So Bobby played like a demon. He seemed to get better with every game. And each time, he did something that amazed the fans, many of whom came from neighboring towns just to see him perform. Bobby always searched the stands for signs of a scout, but he really couldn't tell.

Then, near the end of the season, came a game against Dewersville. All Bobby did in that one was belt three home runs and a double, drive in eight, and make two great catches in the outfield. He was a storybook high school player, all right, but by now he was really beginning to think that no one important would ever see him play.

After the game, he was talking to Josh and a couple of other boys when a wrinkled, old black man tapped him on the shoulder.

"Could I talk to you a minute, Bobby?" the man asked in a steady, strong voice.

Bobby turned. At first he thought the man was just going to tell him what a good game he had played. People did that all the time now. But no matter how many fans and parents came up to him, Bobby was always friendly. So he nodded and smiled at the stranger, then told his friends he'd see them in a few minutes.

"I'm Barney Rogers," the man said, putting out his hand. "And I'm a scout for the San Francisco Giants."

Bobby's mouth dropped. For a second he didn't know what to say. He looked at the grey-haired man smiling at him. Then, he remembered.

"You're not *the* Barney Rogers? The great ballplayer?"

The old man chuckled. "It's not too many from your generation who know me from my playing days."

"I've read all about those New York Giants teams of the '50s, the rivalry with the old Brooklyn Dodgers and the Yankees."

"Yep. The game really lost something when the Giants and Dodgers moved to the West Coast."

"And you're a scout now," Bobby said, still trying to take it all in.

"That's right, son. I never left the organization. When my playing days ended, I coached for awhile, then decided to scout. That's what I like best, finding kids who can really play the game.

"How did you find me? I mean, way out here? Did Coach Tuttle call you or something?"

"It's a long story," the old man said. "But I've seen you play three or four times this year. Just was waiting for the right time to meet you."

Barney Rogers had a quick smile that made his brow wrinkle even more. His skin had a rugged leathery look from all the hours in the sun and wind, playing or watching ballgames. But there was a sparkle in his eye that said he loved every minute of his work and loved talking to young ballplayers.

"Look, do you have a little more time so we can talk?" Barney asked.

Bobby looked over at Josh and the other boys. They were already kind of backing away. It was as if Bobby were about to enter a world where they didn't belong, didn't belong at all.

"Sure," Bobby said quickly. He had been dreaming about this moment for years and wasn't about to let it get away. "Why don't we go sit over there on the bleachers?"

"Lead the way, son."

Bobby stopped to introduce Barney to Coach Tuttle, who was putting the game gear into a large duffel bag. The two men shook hands and grinned. As Barney and Bobby started walking again, Bobby felt the old man's arm on his shoulder.

"You've got a lot of natural talent," Barney said quietly, in a fatherly tone. "I've seen a lot of ball-players in my time, and right now you stack up with the best of them for your age."

Bobby couldn't believe his ears. After all this time wondering how good he was, Bobby was now listening to a scout for the San Francisco Giants tell him he was one of the best! And that could mean only one thing. He felt his heart pounding with excitement.

The two sat down on the bleachers. Bobby

looked out over the field. He thought of all the players who had gone to Caldwell High before him. None had ever gone on to play professional baseball. Suddenly, he found himself wondering again if he could do it at all.

"Don't know what to say, eh Bobby?" Barney said. "I can understand that. But you must know why I'm here, and I'm sure you have a ton of questions."

"To tell you the truth, I've been waiting for this moment for a long time," Bobby confided. "And now that it's here, I don't know what to say. I've always tried to be the best player I could be. But playing here in Caldwell, I was never sure how good that was."

"Well, you can take it from me. You're very good. I must see a couple of hundred ballplayers for every one I talk to. And of those, maybe one in fifty ever gets a minor league contract."

Bobby took a deep breath and swallowed hard. He wasn't quite sure just where he fit in. But he couldn't stand waiting any longer. He had to know.

"Are you saying, Mr. Rogers, that I'm good enough to play in the minor leagues?"

"No, Bobby, I'm not," the scout said, and the youngster's heart sank. "What I'm saying is that I think you're good enough to play in the *major leagues!*"

4

Bobby Blaine ran all the way home. It didn't matter that he lived nearly three miles from the ballfield. He would have run even if it were ten miles. He couldn't wait to tell his parents what had happened. And also that Barney Rogers wanted to talk with them right away.

Bobby was breathless when he arrived at his house. Because of the game and his talk with the scout, it was nearly dinner time. Lewis Blaine was already home from his insurance agency, and Linda Blaine was putting the finishing touches on a chicken dinner. But everything stopped when their son burst through the kitchen door.

"Mom, Dad," Bobby gasped. "You're not gonna believe what happened today, not in a million years."

"You broke another record," Lewis Blaine said, matter-of-factly. He was used to his son's baseball success.

"Lewis!" said Bobby's mother quickly. "Don't act like a new record is something that happens every day."

"With Bobby it does," his father said. "What

was it this time, son? I didn't mean to make it sound as if I didn't care."

Bobby laughed in between still trying to catch his breath. "You'll care, all right," he said. "There was a major league scout at the game today. From the San Francisco Giants. And he wants to give me a contract!"

Mr. Blaine stood up and looked squarely at his son, who was already about an inch taller than he was.

"A contract?" he asked. "A professional contract? Are you sure? Why do they want to sign you now when you still have another year of high school? Do they want to send you to some kind of rookie league for the summer?"

"Slow down, dear," Mrs. Blaine said. She was the calm one in the house. And she always liked to hear both sides of the story. "Let Bobby talk before you go asking all those questions."

"It's okay, Mom," Bobby said. "All the questions in the world still won't make this seem real. The Giants don't want me to go to a rookie league, and they don't want me to go to the minor leagues. Dad, the Giants want me now. They want me for the majors, for the Giants."

Mr. Blaine sat down again, staring at his son as he did. "The majors," he said, then repeated it, this time as a question. "The majors?"

"The majors," Bobby answered. "The big leagues. The San Francisco Giants!"

"No, it can't be," Lewis Blaine said slowly. "It's

got to be some kind of mistake. You must have heard wrong."

"No, I didn't, Dad," said Bobby, his voice getting higher. "Mr. Rogers told me."

"Bobby, you're barely 17 years old," his father said. "You have another year of high school. You've never been away from home before. I don't want to ruin this for you, but it has to be a mistake. Don't you see? It has to be."

Mr. Blaine just shook his head. He looked upset. Maybe someone was playing a cruel joke on his son. Maybe a couple of the boys. What if they got some guy to say he was a scout? Mrs. Blaine walked over and put her hand on her husband's shoulder.

"I think your father is right, Bobby," she said. "How can they take a high school junior and put him right into the big leagues? I know it's something you've always dreamed about. Maybe because you want it so badly your mind played a little trick on you."

"A little trick?" Bobby said, almost yelling. "Well, if you don't believe *me*, maybe you'll believe Mr. Rogers."

But even while he was talking, Bobby began to wonder whether he had gotten things mixed up. Could it be that his parents were right?

"Who's Mr. Rogers?" his father asked.

"The scout. The scout from the Giants. He used to be a big league ballplayer, and he's coming over to the house to talk to you after dinner."

Lewis and Linda Blaine looked at each other. They knew something was up. Bobby wasn't the kind of boy who made up stories. He never had been. Now he was telling them some scout wanted to give him a major league contract. It seemed impossible. How could it happen?

Bobby was standing by the window. It looked as if there might be tears in his eyes. Neither Mr. nor Mrs. Blaine knew quite what to say to him. They would just have to wait and see whether this Mr. Rogers showed up, and if he did, listen to what he had to say.

5

Dinner was a disaster. No one really ate anything. Mrs. Blaine said they would be having leftovers tomorrow. Though she said it with a smile, no one laughed. Then, at about 7:30, the doorbell rang. Bobby answered it. Sure enough, Barney Rogers was standing there, a smile on his wrinkled face. Bobby brought him inside and introduced the scout to his parents.

"You're really a scout for the San Francisco Giants?" Mr. Blaine asked.

"Last time I looked, and that goes back a long way," Barney Rogers said. "But I do have a card here that . . ."

As he talked, the scout pulled out his wallet and began to open it, but Lewis Blaine held up his hand.

"No need to do that, Mr. Rogers."

"Please, it's Barney."

"All right, Barney. It's just that Bobby's story really took us by surprise. You can't really blame us for wondering. Come in and sit down."

They gathered around the kitchen table. Mrs. Blaine poured coffee for the men and herself. For a few seconds, no one spoke, but Barney Rogers broke the silence by coming right to the point.

"What Bobby told you is true," he said thoughtfully. "We think Bobby has major league ability right now, and we would like to bring him up right away if he signs a contract."

"I really find this hard to believe," Mr. Blaine said. "Bobby just turned 17. He has played baseball all his life, but only here in Caldwell. Sure, he's a whole lot better than the other boys here. But what does that really prove? Caldwell High is about as close to the major leagues as home movies are to Hollywood."

The old scout nodded. "I can understand how you feel," he said. "But you have to understand me. I've been looking at young players all my life, and I can tell when a kid has the real goods. Bobby is the best prospect I've ever seen. I've been watching him for a year, and I think he's ready."

Then Barney smiled. "You know, in some ways your son reminds me a bit of myself. I was just about his age when the Giants found me. Luckily, that was the same year Jackie Robinson began playing for the Dodgers, so black players were finally in the majors. The one difference is that Bobby's better."

"But even if you're right, Barney, and Bobby is as good as you say, why not try him in the minors first, where there isn't any pressure?"

"Good question, Mr. Blaine," the scout said. "Under normal conditions, that's just what we'd do. But the new owners of the Giants have pledged to build a winning team. We already have some fine young players. But we don't have a strong centerfielder. We bring Bobby up now, in June, and we let him finish the season. Then we'll all know better where we stand. But don't get me wrong. This isn't some kind of stunt to bring fans in. We want Bobby because we think he can help us win."

"What about school?" Mrs. Blaine asked. "He hasn't even finished high school."

"I know this whole thing must seem sudden and strange," Barney said. "But Bobby should be back to resume school in the fall."

"Come on, Mr. Rogers," said Bobby's father, forgetting to call the scout Barney. It was easy to see he was concerned. "You know as well as I do that something could happen. What if the team wants Bobby to play winter ball? And what about next year? Spring training starts in March, whether he's in the majors or the minors. He won't even have a chance to graduate from high school."

"In that case, the Giants would provide tutors. We would guarantee that Bobby would finish high school."

"I think we're all forgetting something," Mrs. Blaine said. "Nobody has asked Bobby what he wants to do. After all, it's his life we're talking about."

The two men looked at each other. Then all three adults looked at Bobby, who had been sitting there quietly listening to everyone else discuss his future. He took a deep breath, then got up from the table and left the room. Everyone thought that maybe he had heard enough and needed time to think it over. But in a few seconds he was back, and he had a small, weather-beaten bat in his hands.

"See this bat, Mr. Rogers?" he asked, running his hands up and down the rough wood. "I've had this bat since I was six years old. I learned to hit with it. And I always used it to hit stones in the backyard. Sometimes for hours on end.

"And all the time I did that I was making believe I was in the big leagues. I pretended to be all my favorite players. Or I pretended to be myself, hitting a home run to win the world series, or any big game. All I ever wanted was to play big league baseball."

Bobby looked at the old bat, and for a second he actually started to take a cut. Then he realized where he was and stopped himself. No one said a word, but Mrs. Blaine seemed to dab at her eyes with a napkin. Finally, Mr. Blaine broke the silence.

"Are you saying you want to go to the Giants?" he asked.

"How can I not go?" was Bobby's instant reply.

6

There were about three weeks between Barney Rogers' visit to Caldwell and the end of the school year. And they became the busiest three weeks of Bobby Blaine's life. There was just so much to do. He finished the baseball season and was once again the best player in the league. Along the way, he had to study for final exams. But during this time there was something else on his mind. And it was there every minute of the day.

He, Bobby Blaine, was going to the major leagues. And it would be happening within a few short weeks. He wondered what it would be like, that is, what it would *really* be like. As he lay in bed trying to sleep one night, he thought about the Giants and about playing in San Francisco.

The team was in third place in its division. The Giants had some fine players, like shortstop Luke Blanton, catcher Roger Sarason, first baseman Tommy Ardmore, and veteran rightfielder Willie Stockton. They also had some outstanding pitchers in starters Bob Williams and Jackie Ross and reliever Milt "Dial-An-Out" Bell. Manager Gus Hardnet was a seasoned baseball man who ran a tight ship, at least that's what the newspapers said.

Bobby also knew from the papers that center-fielder Ricky Tolbert was having a terrible year. Tolbert was in his third season. At first, many said he was a coming superstar. But each year his hitting got worse and worse. So far this year his batting average was hovering around the .200 mark, and for the first time, it was affecting his play in the field. And that's why the Giants wanted Bobby Blaine.

"How can I take Ricky Tolbert's place?" Bobby questioned out loud, without even thinking. It was the first time he had real doubts about going. Then he thought about San Francisco. The big city. The only time he had ever left Caldwell was to visit his grandparents in Culver City, some 40 miles south. And what about his teammates? How would they accept a 17-year-old suddenly being thrown in with them?

It was his first sleepless night, and there would probably be others. He didn't tell his parents the way he felt. If they knew, they might not let him go. Josh was the only one he talked to about it. His best friend tried to help, but there wasn't much he could say. Because he couldn't put himself in Bobby's shoes, Josh had a hard time understanding how Bobby felt.

About a week before school ended, Barney Rogers returned to Caldwell. This time he brought someone with him. It was John Denholm, the Giants' general manager. They had with them a contract, which they talked over with Bobby's parents and the family lawyer. Everyone agreed it was fair. Mr. Blaine, Mrs. Blaine, and their son, all signed.

———

"Fifty thousand dollars!" Josh said, his eyes almost bugging out of his head. "What in the world will you do with fifty grand?"

"That's just my signing bonus," Bobby answered, a smile on his face. "I get another fifty in salary for playing the rest of the season."

"You've gotta be kidding," Josh said. He knew they paid ballplayers a lot of money, but somehow he never thought Bobby would get that much.

Neither did Bobby. "It surprised me, too," he said. "Of course, my parents are putting it in a trust fund until I'm 18, but I want to give some of it to them."

"What about buying a Mercedes?" Josh asked. "Isn't that what all the ballplayers do nowadays?"

Bobby laughed. "Not this ballplayer. Can you see me driving into Caldwell in a Mercedes?"

"Yeah, a pink and purple one."

"Afraid not. I'm still more of a Chevy man, a sharp pickup," said Bobby.

"Only if I ride shotgun," Josh said.

"Any time."

"Then I give you permission to buy the truck."

"Next year."

The two boys laughed, and for a few minutes Bobby was able to forget about leaving home. But time was getting short. The boys had been walking toward Boswell's as they talked. Right before they got there, Josh spotted another friend across the street.

"Hey, there's Dave Morse," he said. "He's got some stuff of mine. Grab a table while I chase him down."

Josh took off as he spoke. Bobby went inside, bought a paper, sat down, and turned to the sports page. He looked for any news of the Giants. They had lost to the Dodgers, 5-3, as Ricky Tolbert struck out to end the game with the tying runs in scoring position. Bobby almost smiled but caught himself. He didn't want to be happy over someone else's failure, but he also knew that if Tolbert kept playing poorly, he'd have more of a chance to get in there right away.

As he read, he didn't even notice that someone had sat down beside him.

"Hi, Bobby, want some company?" a soft voice asked.

Bobby looked up quickly. It was Carol Pendergast, a pretty junior at Caldwell High who was in several of Bobby's classes. In fact, once they had gone to a party together. Carol had asked him. But because baseball and studies took nearly all of his time, he rarely dated.

"Hi," he said nervously, looking around for Josh. But his friend wasn't in sight. Carol pushed her long, blonde hair off her cheek and smiled. Bobby could feel himself blush. He fumbled with the paper, then put it down. Carol was just looking at him.

"I hear you're about to become a real celebrity," she said finally. "Everybody in town is talking about it. You really must be excited."

"I guess so," Bobby said, without much life in his voice.

"Bobby Blaine," Carol said in a teasing tone. "I thought all you ever wanted was to be a big league ballplayer. It's all you talked about when we went to Roz's party."

"Yeah, well now that it's happening it's a little scary. Going to California and all that. It'll be a big change."

"From what I've read about San Francisco, you can really have a good time there."

"I'm going there to play ball, Carol," he said. "There's not gonna be much time for fun."

"That's your trouble, Bobby, you never leave any room for fun. You should once in a while, you know. Everyone needs that."

Bobby took a deep breath. In a way, Carol was right. But he also knew that baseball was enough fun for him, and he didn't think she'd understand that. Baseball had always been the most fun. He saw no reason why that should change.

"Anyway, I bet you can afford to buy a girl a soda now," she added with a smile. "I'm kind of thirsty."

"Oh, yeah, sure." Bobby left and soon returned with two Cokes. When he got there, Josh was sitting alongside Carol.

"One more, please," Josh said, as if Bobby were the waiter.

"You got it," Bobby answered, glad that his friend had arrived.

The three chatted for about a half-hour as they sipped their drinks. They talked about school, about other friends, and of course, about Bobby going to the Giants. Both Carol and Josh asked him about the money he would make and if he thought he might end up a millionaire.

That kind of talk made Bobby uneasy. He had never thought much about money before. Now, everybody seemed to be thinking about it. As he walked home he thought about the money some more. He was about to have fifty thousand dollars in the bank, with more on the way. Would it change him? Would it change the way others treated him? The more he thought about going to the Giants, the more questions he seemed to have.

And as he neared home, it dawned on him that his life might never again be quite the same.

7

Finally, the big day arrived. Barney Rogers was in Caldwell the night before and stayed with the Blaines. The next morning Bobby said goodbye to his mother and Josh. The two boys gave each other a quick hug. Then his father drove Bobby and Barney to the airport in Des Moines, where he said goodbye. Lewis Blaine had wanted to go all the way to San Francisco with them. But Bobby had said it wouldn't look right for a new major leaguer to have his father bring him, like he was a new kid at camp.

The flight was smooth, but Bobby's stomach wasn't. He was nervous. Barney Rogers could sense it and tried to calm him. But he knew the kid would have to feel his own way through.

They landed at the airport in San Francisco, where a car was waiting to take them to the ballpark. This is it, Bobby thought. In just a short time, I'll be a Giant. He almost caught himself saying ''Wow!'' But there was no time for wows. It was time for business.

''The team gets back from its road trip tonight,'' Barney said after they got in the car. ''And we play the Braves next. The plan is for you to work out with the team for two or three days, then we'll add you to the roster. Sound all right?''

"I guess so," Bobby answered, as he stared out the car window at the buildings and people they passed. He felt a pang of homesickness come over him. He wondered what Josh was doing, and even found himself thinking about Carol Pendergast. Maybe he should have asked her out, he thought.

"You okay, son?" Barney asked.

"Just a little nervous. This is a pretty big step."

"Don't blame you. It's gonna take you a while to relax. But if I didn't think you had the ability to handle the pressure, I never would have gone through with this. Gus and the coaches will give you a lot of help, and the rest of the guys aren't bad. You'll get tested, and there will be some teasing. A couple of guys may not like you at first, but that always happens when 24 guys are thrown together. You've got to try not to let that stuff bother you. Just play baseball the way I know you can."

"Easier said than done," Bobby replied.

As the driver turned off the freeway, Bobby caught a glimpse of the stadium and thought about playing baseball in Candlestick Park. From what he had read, it wasn't an easy place to play. The winds there were almost legendary, and the nights were often cold. Though the Giants had had several lean years, the team was now in the process of rebuilding. The current season wasn't quite at the halfway mark, and the team was just seven games out of first.

After they parked, Bobby and Barney made their way through the stadium. Bobby looked wide-eyed at the huge ballpark. The field, with natural grass, looked beautiful to him. So did the locker rooms below. There were familiar names above each locker: Blanton, Ross, Stockton, Ardmore, Tolbert. And at the end of the line . . . Blaine.

What a thrill it was to see his name there. He met the equipment manager, Doc Hardy, who gave him a uniform with number 42 and the rest of his gear.

"Try it on," Barney said. "Let's see how you look."

It didn't take Bobby more than a couple of minutes to get into the uniform. And when he looked into a full-length mirror at the end of the locker room, he couldn't believe his eyes.

"I'm not a kid anymore," he said to himself. "I'm a major league ballplayer, just what I always wanted to be."

He found himself smiling broadly. Right now he felt as if he could hit .400. He was a major leaguer, and he didn't want it any other way.

8

The team got back in town about 8 p.m. Bobby was waiting at the stadium with Barney and met everyone when they checked in. The players were anxious to get home after the long road trip, and no one really took time to say much to him.

Manager Hardnet, however, asked Bobby to step into his office. Hardnet had been the Giants' skipper for five years now. He was a veteran baseball man with an unsmiling face and a slight pot belly. He had been a catcher during his playing days and a tough one at that. All he asked was that his players give 100 percent and not make mistakes. And now he was also asking them to win.

"Might as well tell you right out, Blaine, I was the last one to agree to this thing," he said gruffly. "You're too young and I don't see how you can be ready for the Bigs. But I was outvoted, and you're here. So I won't fool around with you. I'm putting you in centerfield, and you're gonna have to show me what you can do. And fast. Otherwise, I'll live with Tolbert out there."

"Gus, you're scarin' the kid," Barney said.

"Why shouldn't I? He's got to know what he's

31

up against and what I expect."

"I wouldn't want it any other way," Bobby said. "If I can't make it, I don't want to take up space here. So if things don't work out, I'm ready to go to the minors."

"Okay, kid," the manager said slowly. "I like the way you think. That's a good start. Tomorrow's an off-day but we work out at 10:00. Friday the Braves come in. I'll give you a day on the bench to adjust. Saturday you start."

Bobby nodded, still not sure whether he liked his manager or not. But Barney had said Gus Hardnet was a fair man, and that was good enough. All he wanted was a chance.

"You tell him he's roomin' with Coop?" the manager asked Barney.

"No, I wasn't sure what you were gonna do."

"We sent Dugan out." The manager then walked to the door and opened it. "Coop, get in here."

Another young man entered. He couldn't have been more than a few years older than Bobby.

"Jeff Cooper, Bobby Blaine," the manager said. "You guys are roomies. Coop, don't lead the kid astray."

Bobby knew Jeff Cooper was a utility infielder who didn't play much. He was 22 years old and the youngest player on the team after Bobby. The two shook hands, though neither smiled. Big league baseball, Bobby thought. It was sure a strange way to start.

"You got a car?" Jeff asked.

"I don't drive," Bobby replied.

"You what?"

"I don't drive. I was planning to get my license this summer. Most places in Caldwell are within walking or running distance."

"Caldwell, huh?" Jeff said. "All right, come on with me."

"See you tomorrow, Bobby," Barney said.

"Thanks for everything, Mr. Rogers," Bobby answered.

"Workout's at 10:00 sharp," was all Manager Hardnet said.

9

Jeff Cooper hardly spoke as he drove through the crowded city streets toward his apartment in North Beach. Bobby felt very much alone. He was in the big city with no friends. In fact, the only friendly face was Barney's. Neither Manager Hardnet nor Jeff Cooper had so much as smiled.

"This wasn't my idea," Jeff said coldly. "I just want you to know that. Billy Dugan was a good friend, and they dumped him to bring you up. Then they tell me you're my new roommate. Nothing like freedom of choice, huh?"

Bobby wasn't sure what to say. All his life he had been around friendly people. He couldn't think of Josh talking to someone like this. Not even Steve Ferris. He wondered if everyone was going to act this way.

Bobby realized, of course, that joining the Giants would affect Ricky Tolbert, but he hadn't known about Billy Dugan being sent down or rooming with Jeff.

"I hope you're not gonna cramp my style, kid," Jeff continued. "I know a couple of girls who come around, and you better not scare them off. They're probably gonna think I have my baby brother living with me."

Jeff just shook his head and kept driving. Bobby had nothing to say. When they arrived at the apartment building, Bobby got his suitcases out of the trunk and carried them inside. Jeff didn't offer to help. The apartment was small and sloppy: clothes thrown all over, records and tapes lying near the stereo, dirty dishes in the sink. For a second, Bobby wished his mother would come and clean up the place.

"That's your room there. Billy left some crap around. Shove it under the bed or something. Maybe I'll get lucky and they'll bring him back before the season ends."

Bobby went into his room and unpacked. There was just a bed, dresser, and small desk. The closet had some dirty clothes on the floor and he pushed them into a corner. When Bobby went back into the living room, Jeff was reading a book and sipping a beer.

"I know this is a stupid question, but if you want a beer, just help yourself," Jeff said. And before Bobby could say anything, Jeff said, "Don't tell me. You don't drink. What *do* you do?"

For the first time, Bobby felt himself getting angry. He was going slow, trying to be nice. But he knew he couldn't take much more of Jeff. He went back into his room and wrote a letter home. When Bobby came back out, Jeff was drinking another beer and watching television. And as

Bobby started past him on the way to the kitchen, Jeff put his foot out.

"Why the hell did they bother to bring up a green kid like you?" Jeff asked, shaking his head in disgust.

"Suppose you come out to the ballpark tomorrow and find out," Bobby snapped back. "That is, if you're sober enough."

Bobby started toward the kitchen, but Jeff jumped up and grabbed his arm.

"Who do you think you're talking to like that?" Jeff demanded.

Bobby whirled around and with a single motion shook Jeff's arm loose. Jeff began to raise his hands, but before he could move, Bobby had a grip on both his wrists. Jeff could feel the raw power in Bobby's hands, and he realized the 17-year-old standing in front of him was very strong.

"I don't like this any more than you do, Jeff," Bobby said. "I didn't ask to room with you, and I didn't send Billy Dugan to the minors. If you feel you've got to blame me, fine. But let me tell you one thing. Where I come from you don't put your hands on someone unless you intend to do something."

Bobby's cold stare told Jeff he meant business. Jeff backed off.

"Okay, we'll see how good you are tomorrow, hotshot," Jeff said. "I'm going to bed. Make sure you're ready to leave by 9:15."

"I'll be ready."

10

On the way to the ballpark, Jeff Cooper was quiet again. At least he had stopped the wise remarks. When they reached Candlestick Park, Bobby looked for Barney Rogers' friendly face. He wasn't there. In the locker room some of the players gave Bobby a quick hello. A few shook his hand or slapped him on the back. Bobby even heard a couple of players say "good luck, kid," and he felt a little better.

"Ready to play, kid?" someone asked. It was Manager Hardnet, in his usual, unsmiling way.

"I hope so," Bobby answered. "Where's Mr. Rogers?"

"Where do you think?" a nearby player chirped, "on his television show!"

"Don't listen to the wiseguys," the manager said. "None of 'em are as smart as they think they are. Barney had to hustle off to Nebraska to look at a couple of kids. He never stays around here for long. He was called out this morning."

But before Bobby could think about his only friend leaving, Hardnet spoke again.

"This is our batting coach, Irv Randall," the

skipper said. "He'll watch you in the cage today. Irv knows his business, so listen to him."

After chatting with the coach for a few minutes, Bobby finished dressing and went out onto the field. He looked up at the empty seats, an awesome sight. From the field, the stadium seemed huge. Bobby tried to picture what it would be like to have some 50,000 fans up there cheering for him. That was tough. But just being out on a field again was a good feeling. Now he felt he was on an equal footing with everyone else.

He did his warmups, then went out to centerfield to shag flies. Ricky Tolbert was standing nearby but said nothing. Bobby could see the other centerfielder watching him out of the corner of his eye several times. Finally, it was Bobby's turn to hit.

Bobby grabbed his bat and dug in, but when he looked out at the mound, batting practice pitcher Chuck Herbert was gone and Jackie Ross was standing there. Ross was one of the Giants' best pitchers, a hard-throwing right-hander who wasn't afraid to put the ball under a batter's chin.

"Jackie needs some work and so do you," said Hardnet. "Just relax in there and take your cuts."

"If they want a show, I'll give 'em one," Bobby said to himself. He could almost feel the energy begin to flow through his body. His hands tightened on the bat, and he stared out at Ross. Bobby had the same good feeling he always had at Caldwell High. In other words, he was ready.

Sure enough, Ross's first pitch was high and tight. Bobby backed off but didn't flinch. He dug in again and Ross threw. This one was on the outside corner, and Bobby calmly stepped into it and stroked a line drive to rightfield. Next, he timed a curve and whacked it down the leftfield line. He popped up a change but then caught a slider and drove it to the wall on one hop.

By now, almost the entire team was around the cage and watching. A few of the players were shouting to him, urging him on. He was stinging the ball now, and he felt better and better with each swing.

Jackie Ross was sweating, throwing harder. But this kid was hitting him with ease, and some of the players were beginning to get on Jackie. Finally, he fired one at Bobby's head, barely missing him. The kid hit the dirt hard but bounced right back up, glaring at the pitcher.

Ross was rubbing up a new ball as if nothing had happened. He got set again, but so did Bobby. The pitch was a fastball, belt high. Bobby swung from his heels and crushed it. He had that good feeling right up his arms and into his shoulders. The ball flew high and deep toward leftcenter. It cleared the outfield fence and landed halfway up the bleachers, well over 400 feet from home plate.

The other players couldn't believe what they had just seen. Now they knew that Bobby Blaine wasn't there as a gimmick to attract fans. He was there because he could hit a baseball, and hit it a long way. His age didn't really matter. It shouldn't have mattered in the first place.

Jackie Ross walked off the field, mumbling something about it not being his day. And when Chuck Herbert returned to the mound, Bobby kept hitting line drives. Before Bobby was through, he belted another pair into the far corners of the stands. Many of his new teammates let him know they were on his side and glad to have him as part of the team. This was more like it.

When practice ended, Bobby went back to the outfield and began running back and forth from center to left, then from center to right. The others had gone in, but Bobby didn't care. There were still some things he had to do to get ready for Saturday. He was working hard and didn't see the other player jog out to him.

"Whatcha doin', kid, running wind sprints? I got to do some extra running, too. At my age you need all the running you can get."

"No, I'm counting steps," Bobby said to Willie Stockton, almost without thinking.

Stockton was nearly 38 years old and coming to the end of a fine career. He had joined the Giants in a trade six years ago. His former team had thought he was beginning to fade, but he fooled them. As a Giant, he produced some of his finest seasons ever. He was the closest thing to a superstar the Giants had seen in recent years. But this season he was just hitting in the .270s, and his power was down. He looked to be close to the end

"Whaddaya mean, counting steps?" the thin black man asked Bobby.

"Just getting used to the outfield. Trying to judge the distance from my starting position to the warning track, the track to the wall, and the amount of space in the gaps."

"You don't fool around, do you?" Stockton said smiling.

"I just want to be ready," answered Bobby. "I don't like to make mistakes."

"I can see that. You know, a lot of the guys were pretty ticked off when they heard you were coming in, and not even out of high school yet," the veteran said.

"I could tell," Bobby said, "but I don't really see why."

"They thought it was a stunt, a way for the Giants to get some ink and some more fans. But a lot of us still think we have a chance to win it."

"Why not?" Bobby asked. "The Mets were only eight years old when they won in '69."

"So they were," Stockton said. "You know your baseball, all right. And I'm beginning to get the feeling you can play the game, too."

"I try," Bobby said.

"Your little show in the batting cage didn't hurt, either. Jackie Ross wasn't too happy when you took him downtown."

Bobby laughed. He liked Willie Stockton, and he was glad the veteran outfielder was being so nice to him.

"Just go slow with the guys," Stockton said. "Most of them will come around. You win a few games for us and I know they will."

"Thanks for the advice," Bobby said.

"Don't mention it," Stockton said.

Bobby took a deep breath and finished his workout. Then he watched Willie Stockton, running hard along the outfield track. He knew the veteran didn't have many years left. And he wondered if his own career would last as long.

11

Bobby slept well that night. He had spent about an hour on the phone with his parents, telling them everything that had happened. Jeff Cooper still hadn't said much to him, hadn't even talked about Bobby's hitting. But Bobby didn't really care. Hitting Jackie Ross so well had really made him feel he could play in the big leagues. Now all he wanted was to get in his first game.

The next night the Giants went up against the Braves, who were in town for a four-game series. Bobby was on the bench. But just being part of a big league game was exciting enough. He had even hit a couple more into the seats during batting practice. Now he tried to keep his mind on the game, but he couldn't help wondering if he would play.

The Braves had a 4-2 lead in the bottom of the eighth. The Giants were up. With two out, third baseman Ray Marlin singled, and catcher Roger Sarason followed with another base hit. Now Ricky Tolbert, who was batting eighth, was due up.

"Tolbert, get back here," Manager Hardr

shouted. "Blaine, grab your bat and get up there."

For a second, Bobby froze. He was being sent up to pinch-hit in a tough spot. He watched Tolbert come back to the bench and fling his bat in anger.

"Come on, Blaine. Get the lead out!"

Bobby jumped up and grabbed his bat from the rack. He walked out of the dugout and heard the Giants' fans begin to cheer. Then he heard the announcer say: "Your attention, please. Batting for Tolbert, number 42, Bobby Blaine."

Bobby could feel a chill run up his spine. Hearing his name and then the cheer from the large crowd was something he had thought about since he was little. He swung the bat around his head, trying to get loose. A left-hander named Johnny Green was pitching, but now the Braves were making a switch, bringing in their bullpen ace, right-hander Tom Ramsey. Ramsey was a side-armer and tough for righties to hit.

Finally, Bobby dug in. He just wanted to get a piece of the ball, not look foolish. Ramsey's first pitch was a big sidearm curve, and he took it for a ball. His teammates were all yelling now, asking him to get a hit. Next came a fastball, and he watched it for a strike. He took a deep breath and got set again.

Ramsey threw another fastball that rode in on him, but Bobby swung. He hit it off his hands, a pop toward leftfield. The Braves' shortstop ran back and made a nice, over-the-shoulder catch for the third out. Bobby was digging hard around first when the catch was made. He stopped, kicked at the dirt, and returned to the dugout.

"All right, Bobby," said batting coach Irv Randall. "You hung in there against a tough pitcher. He tries to set hitters up for the big curve by using the inside fastball. You'll learn."

A couple of other players gave him a quick pat on the back as they headed out for the field. But he thought he heard a voice say, "It ain't that easy, huh, hotshot?" He looked around but couldn't tell who said it. He grabbed his mitt and played center in the top of the ninth, but no ball came his way, and the Braves hung on for the victory.

It wasn't until later that it really hit him. He had showered and was getting ready to leave when he thought to himself: "I did it. I just played in a major league baseball game."

12

After the game, Manager Hardnet told Bobby that the plans hadn't changed. He would be starting in center the next day. The skipper also told him something else.

"As far as I'm concerned, we're in a pennant race," Hardnet had said. "I think we have a chance to win. You help us, you'll play. If not, we'll get someone else out there. I'm not trying to put extra pressure on you; I'm just telling you the way it is. I can see you've got the ability. It's just a question of whether you're ready to put it together."

"Thanks for the advice," Bobby had said.

He thought about it all night. Having a roommate who hardly spoke to him didn't help much, either. That night, he put a call through to Josh.

"It's me," Bobby said, glad to hear the sound of his friend's voice.

"Gee, I thought you had forgotten about your old friends now that you're a big baseball star."

"Cut the crap, Josh, I'm not in the mood."

Josh sensed his friend was serious.

"Hey, what's up,?" he asked. "I figured you'd

be on cloud nine by now. You're still starting tomorrow, aren't you?"

"Supposed to," Bobby said. "It's just that . . . I miss you guys. Even Ferris. There's really no one here to talk to."

"I pictured you talking baseball with just about everyone you met."

"Talking baseball's one thing. But I don't have any real friends here."

"Well, you just need a little time," Josh said. "What about your roommate?"

"Cooper? He's a prime candidate for a smack in the mouth. He came close once already."

"You kiddin'? What's his problem?"

"He blames me because his old roomie was sent down to make room for me on the roster."

"Oh, boy You got to deal with that kind of stuff, too?"

"Well, it's his problem. I've got to worry about playing centerfield. That's my job and it has to come first."

"Job? What happened to fun?" Josh asked. "I never saw a guy have as much fun playing baseball as you."

Bobby laughed. "Yeah, we did have fun. Maybe a few home runs will bring it back. The roughest part so far has been being away from you guys. Think you can make it to a game this year?"

"Gee, I don't know," Josh said. "I'll be working for old man Gaffney again this summer. You know him. Not much time off."

"Some things never change," Bobby said, laughing.

"Can't help it. Some of us still have to work for a living."

"That's not funny, Josh," Bobby said. "I'm not about to apologize because I'm being paid to play baseball."

"Who's asking you to?" Josh said. "But that doesn't change the fact that I have to work. So don't lay a guilt trip on me because I can't run over to Chicago or St. Louis to watch you play."

Bobby couldn't believe what was happening. He had called Josh to hear a friendly voice and now they were almost arguing. He didn't need this the night before his first big-league start.

"Look, Josh. Let's just forget it. I can't seem to say anything right lately."

"Yeah, well, maybe I'm a little touchy, too. Maybe I'm just jealous. But you're right. We've been friends too long for this. Hit one for me tomorrow, okay?"

"I'll try like hell," said Bobby. "See ya."

"See you, pal."

Bobby got ready for bed. As he came out of the bathroom, Jeff Cooper was hanging up the phone.

"Friend of mine's been trying to call for an hour," he snapped. "Why not go a little lighter on the phone, huh?"

"Yeah, fine," Bobby said, not wanting any more arguments.

"Just see that you do."

Now Jeff had gone too far. An angry Bobby whirled around and said, "If I was only hitting .220, I'd have more to worry about than talking to my friends at night. And by the way, wiseguy, you're never gonna hit more than .220 unless you learn not to take your eye off the ball for that split second when you start your stride."

Before Jeff could respond, Bobby turned and walked away. That night Bobby lay in bed for a long time. He thought a lot about the game tomorrow, tried to picture what he'd do in certain situations. But slowly, he found his thoughts drifting to other things. Some of the things Josh had said bothered him. Would baseball become just a job and no longer fun? And why did he expect Josh to drop everything and come running? He should have known better.

The situation with Jeff Cooper was another thing. Bobby knew he couldn't let it go on like this the rest of the season. He was sure his last remark about Jeff's hitting wouldn't improve their relationship. But he had noticed how Jeff always moved his head in a way that might affect his ability to focus on the baseball.

It was late now, and Bobby knew he needed sleep. That was important, too. As he finally drifted off, one last thought went through his mind.

Things had always been much easier back in Caldwell.

13

The next day Bobby was at the ballpark early. He didn't wait for Jeff, just called a cab instead. Doc Hardy was alone in the clubhouse when he got there. Bobby grabbed a soda and sat down on one of the benches.

"Nothing like getting thrown to the wolves," Bobby thought to himself. But he also felt he was ready, as ready as someone his age could be. The locker room was very quiet and he lay down on the bench, staring at the ceiling. He wasn't sure how long he lay there or whether he fell asleep. But he heard footsteps at the other end of the room. At first he thought it was the clubhouse man again. Then he glanced up. Ricky Tolbert was staring down at him.

"You're here early," said the young outfielder, who had recently turned 23.

"Nothing else to do," Bobby answered. It was the first time Tolbert had talked to him. Bobby sat up. "Guess I must have drifted off."

"You're a pretty cool dude. I'll give you that much," Tolbert said. "So you play, I sit."

"I'm sorry," Bobby said, "but I . . ."

Tolbert held up a hand. "Hey, man, it's part of baseball. I ain't blaming you. I'm barely hitting my weight and I'm letting it screw up my whole game. Maybe I can use some time on the pine, and you can climb into the pressure cooker."

Bobby managed a smile. He knew it took guts for Tolbert to talk this way. He wondered how he would act if the shoe were on the other foot.

"Yeah, well just a few weeks ago I was playing for a small high school in Iowa. So this isn't easy for me, either."

"No one said it would be, did they?" Tolbert said. "They can promise the world in this game. And you can make a million bucks. But the bottom line is the same as it was fifty years ago. You got to do the job on the field. I don't care who you are."

"I guess you're right," Bobby said. He was beginning to get butterflies now. A couple of the other players were drifting into the clubhouse. Game time was getting near.

"Look," Ricky Tolbert said. "I don't want to be the enemy. Let me go over some of the Braves' hitters with you. It might help."

The two young players talked for about 15 minutes. Then they got dressed. They talked some more out on the field during warmups. There were more than 45,000 fans on hand when the game began, and many of them had come to see young Bobby Blaine start his first game.

A left-hander named Ronnie Moore was starting for the Braves, while Bob Williams took the hill for the Giants. Bobby was hitting seventh in the lineup. Several of his teammates wished him luck before the game, as did Manager Hardnet. Finally, it was time for the Giants to take the field. The crowd roared, and as Bobby trotted out to centerfield, he felt a high like nothing he had ever felt before.

As the national anthem was playing, Bobby could feel his knees shake. Then the game began, and Bobby tried to keep his mind on the action and nothing else. The first inning passed quickly. But in the second, the Braves' cleanup hitter Max Strawbush belted one to the right centerfield gap.

Bobby took off at the crack of the bat, running as hard as he could. He knew Stockton couldn't reach the ball from his rightfield position. Angling toward the wall and using his great speed, Bobby lunged and reached up at the last second. He caught the ball in the webbing of his glove just as he slammed into the wall.

Despite the impact, he held on. Then he raised his glove in the air to show the ump he had the ball. The crowd went wild, standing and shouting. He had made a great catch, as good as anyone had seen in a long time. And when he came to bat with a runner on second and two down in the bottom half of the inning, he got a standing ovation.

He knew Ronnie Moore liked to throw a hard slider that dipped sharply just before it reached the plate. It wasn't an easy pitch to hit, and Bobby just wanted to make contact. He ran the count to 2-2. Then Moore threw the slider once again.

Bobby stepped into the ball and swung easily. He drove it between short and third into left for a base hit. Ray Marlin scampered home with the first run of the game. Bobby rounded first, then retreated to the bag. The fans gave him another standing ovation. He had gotten a base hit in his second big league at bat. Some of his teammates were calling for the ball. He knew they wanted to give it to him as a souvenir. He felt great.

The Giants went on to win the game, 5-2. Bobby had one other hit, a sixth inning double, and played a solid game in center. In the locker room he got high fives and congrats from almost everyone.

"The bottom line," Ricky Tolbert said. "As long as you keep doing the job."

"That's the name of the game," Bobby said in return.

"You're learning, baby," said Tolbert.

Willie Stockton gave him a high five, then grabbed his arm. Luke Blanton and Tommy Ardmore also grabbed him, and before he could say anything they dragged him into the shower, uniform and all. Bobby laughed and shouted. He loved every minute of it. Baseball was fun again.

Finally, he got dressed and was ready to face the press for the first time. He began wishing his parents could have been there to see him.

14

The press conference lasted about half an hour. Reporters were there from all the Bay Area newspapers, TV and radio stations, and wire services. Most of them asked questions about how Bobby felt playing in the majors at such a young age.

He tried to answer quickly and honestly. In fact, it was hard for him to understand why everyone was making such a fuss.

"I've been playing baseball all my life," he said to one reporter. "I think I'm still going to get a lot better, but I also think I can play here right now. I know one game doesn't really prove anything, so I guess only time will tell. But at 17, I should have the time."

Everyone laughed when he said that. Then another reporter asked Bobby how his new teammates were treating him.

"Pretty good, for the most part," he answered. "But I think some of them look at me as a little brother. You know, the kid who tags along when he isn't always wanted. And some guys might still think I'm here for just, uh, public relations. Maybe a few more base hits will change their minds."

"What about a social life?" another asked. "You can't go to bars, and you're the youngest guy in the league. What are you gonna do for kicks?"

Bobby felt a little uneasy with that one. He shuffled his feet, then coughed twice. Finally, he took a deep breath and answered.

"Well, so far I haven't had time to worry about that. I miss my family and friends. I never did go to bars, so that's not a problem. But it has been a little lonely."

When the press conference ended, Manager Hardnet asked Bobby to come to his office.

"Got a little surprise for you, kid," he said.

Bobby followed his manager into the office. Inside the door he stopped in his tracks, then broke into a huge grin. Sitting on the sofa were his mother and father. The Giants had flown them in to San Francisco for the game. They had been there all the time.

After about five minutes of hugs and kisses, the three of them went out to dinner and then talked into the wee hours of the morning. Bobby stayed with them at their hotel, and they left for Iowa the following afternoon.

Still on a high, Bobby had three hits and two RBIs that night. And the next night, he belted his first major league home run, the game-winning hit in a 6-5 San Francisco victory.

A week later Bobby's batting average was at .381, and he was the toast of baseball. There were requests for interviews and magazine stories, but both his parents and club management felt it was best to wait until the end of the season for that. Besides, the Giants were now in second place, just four games out of first. They had a real chance to win and everybody knew it.

Bobby Blaine continued to play very well. He hit a three-run homer to win one game, and in another got the tying run home by laying down a perfect bunt on a suicide squeeze. He was living with Ricky Tolbert now. Both he and Jeff Cooper had asked for the change. Tolbert was a good friend at the ballpark, but the two didn't really hang out together off the field.

By late August, the Giants were within a game of the front-running Phillies. People were beginning to call them a team of destiny, much like the 1969 New York Mets. And one writer even said the team was being led by a 17-year-old David against all the mighty Goliaths of the National League.

After nearly two months as a big leaguer, Bobby was still hitting .345, with 11 homers and 37 runs batted in. A more perfect script couldn't have come out of Hollywood. In fact, there was already talk of making a movie out of his life. But first things first. The Giants went to Philadelphia for a crucial four-game series with the Phillies. First place was at stake. Bobby and his teammates were sky high.

And that's when it happened.

15

It was the ninth and final inning of the first game. The Giants, on a fifth-inning Bobby Blaine double, had a 3-2 lead behind Jackie Ross. Now they were just three outs away from perhaps the biggest win in the history of the team. Then the first Phils' hitter banged a base hit to left.

The next batter lofted one to right center. Bobby drifted over, ready to make the grab. Suddenly, he thought he heard Willie Stockton holler, "I got it!" Even though it was the centerfielder's ball, for some reason Bobby stopped. The ball dropped between Bobby and Willie, and everyone was safe.

"What happened?" Stockton asked quietly.

"I heard you call it," said Bobby.

"What I said was, 'You got it'!"

Bobby couldn't believe he had heard wrong. He had never made a mistake like that before in his life. He knew these things happened to everyone. But they had never happened to Bobby Blaine.

"Settle down," he said to himself. "There's still a ballgame to be won."

The next batter tried to sacrifice the runners over. But Tommy Ardmore fielded the bunt and threw to Ray Marlin at third for the force. There were now runners on first and second with one out. Manager Hardnet wanted a double play and decided to go to his bullpen ace, Dial-An-Out Bell.

Bell was the Giants' stopper, a crafty right-hander with a tough sinker that batters usually beat into the ground. He was good against both righties and lefties, so he could come in at any time.

A rookie named Art Collum was up. Bell should eat him up, Bobby thought. With the count one and one, Collum went after the sinker and slammed it back through the middle for a base hit. Bobby charged in, hoping to hold the lead runner at third or throw him out at the plate.

He reached down with his gloved hand to scoop the ball and fire it toward the plate. But he came up with . . . nothing. The ball had skipped under his glove and was rolling toward the wall. As it did, the tying run and then the winning run crossed home plate. The Phillies had won the ballgame, 4-3.

You could hear a pin drop in the Giants' locker room. No one spoke. Bobby had left the field almost in a state of shock. Not only had his error cost his team a big ballgame, but he had done something he hadn't done before. He had run through a ball in the outfield, failing to pick it up. When he finally came inside, he just sat in front of his locker and stared at the floor.

"Hey, it's all right, man," Willie Stockton said to him, putting his hand on Bobby's shoulder. "We'll get 'em tomorrow."

Bobby said nothing. Slowly, the players began to drift into the showers, and some chatter finally could be heard again. It didn't make Bobby feel any better.

And it didn't help when Jackie Ross said flatly: "You owe me one, kid. You just cost me a big win."

"Knock it off, man," Willie Stockton said. "The kid feels bad enough. He knows what he did."

"Never hurts to remind them," Ross said angrily. "Then maybe it won't happen again."

"You're forgetting the games he's won for us," Tommy Ardmore added.

"That was then, this is now," said Ray Marlin. "Maybe we just shouldn't ask a boy to do a man's job at crunch time."

The voices were getting angrier. Ardmore and Marlin, Stockton and Ross. Jeff Cooper yelled something, and Ricky Tolbert answered him. For a few seconds a couple of the players seemed close to blows.

"All right, knock it off!" It was Manager Hardnet, and for once Bobby was glad to see him.

"I don't want to hear this kind of crap, not now. Yeah, we lost a ballgame. But we've lost plenty of others. This club has bounced back all year. We'll do it again. So knock off the finger pointing. We win as a team and we lose as a team. And if anyone does any criticizing around here, it's me."

That quieted things. The players slowly left, heading back to the hotel. Bobby was the last to leave. He didn't have a ride. He walked slowly from Veterans Stadium through the streets toward the hotel. He felt alone in a strange place. If he ever needed a friend, it was now. He wasn't sure just how to handle what had just happened to him. His athletic skills had never deserted him before.

He entered the lobby of the hotel. He still wasn't ready to face his teammates. He couldn't. He felt he had let them all down. He had let everyone down. And the reason was simple.

Bobby Blaine had just failed on a baseball field. That was something he had never done before. Not once. Not in all his 17 years.

16

When Bobby got to his room, Ricky Tolbert wasn't there. Bobby remembered something about Ricky having old friends in Philadelphia. He sat down on the bed. Once again he went over the two key plays in his mind. And once again he couldn't believe what he had done. Bobby Blaine just didn't mess things up like that.

He picked up the phone and dialed Josh's number. Josh's mother answered and said he had gone to the movies with Carol Pendergast. Whew. Bobby couldn't believe that one. Josh and Carol. Somehow, it didn't seem right. Josh had never said anything about liking Carol. And everybody knew that Carol had always liked Bobby. It's just that he never really had the nerve to ask her out. And, of course, there was always baseball.

Bobby tried to picture his friends together. He wondered what was playing at the Caldwell Cameo, and what they would do afterward. Then he realized something else. He was jealous. He found himself wishing he were back in Caldwell and at the movies with Carol. For a split second it even crossed his mind that he'd rather be doing that than playing centerfield for the San Francisco Giants.

He tried calling his parents but got no answer. Where could they be? Was everyone deserting him? His parents, his best friend. Didn't they know he needed them, that he had made a costly error in a big game?

Bobby was almost angry. He just didn't want to be alone with nothing to do. He went back downstairs to the hotel lobby. None of his teammates were around. He even looked into the bar. Manager Hardnet was sitting there, talking to Irv Randall and another coach. They were all sipping beer. Bobby figured they probably wouldn't want to talk to him.

He sat down in the lobby and looked around. For a few minutes he fumbled with a magazine. Nothing changed his mood. He wasn't even thinking about tomorrow's game, which would be on national television. Instead he was thinking about Bobby Blaine and why he was so unhappy.

Then he noticed some people enter the lobby. It looked like a family just checking in for the night. There were four of them: the mother and father, a boy about nine, and a girl who looked about his age. She had long brown hair and a nice smile. In fact, she looked a little bit like Carol.

They stood at the desk for a few minutes as the father talked to the clerk. There seemed to be some kind of problem. Finally, they sat down on a sofa near Bobby. After about five minutes the father talked to the clerk again, then he and his wife went into the bar, leaving the two children in the lobby.

Bobby took a deep breath and went over to them.

"Hi," he said. "Are you staying at this hotel?"

The girl looked as if she wasn't sure whether she should talk to him. But Bobby smiled and she found herself smiling, too.

"We were supposed to, but there was some kind of mix-up and now we're not sure if we're going to have a room or not."

"My name's Bobby Blaine," he said, sitting down.

"I'm Janet Moreland, and this is my brother, Jimmy."

"Hey, Jimmy."

"Hi," the young boy said yawning. He looked very tired.

"Where are you from?" Bobby asked.

"We're from Cambridge, Massachusetts," Janet said. "We're on our way to Kentucky to visit relatives. But my parents wanted to show us Philadelphia, so we were planning to spend a couple of days here. Are you with your family, too?"

"Not exactly," Bobby said. He almost didn't want to say he was a ballplayer, but Janet looked puzzled.

"I'm with the San Francisco Giants," he said.

With that, Janet's brother perked up. "The baseball team! Wow! Are you a bat boy?"

"No, I'm a player."

Janet looked as if she thought he were handing her a line.

"Honest," he said. "I play for the Giants."

"What do you play?" Jimmy asked.

"Centerfield," Bobby said, again thinking about his error just a few hours earlier.

"I don't understand," Janet said. "Aren't the Giants a major league team?"

Bobby laughed, nodding his head. "It's a long story."

"How old are you?" she asked.

"Seventeen."

"I'll be 17 in October," she said smiling.

Just then Janet's mother and father returned.

"Everything all right here?" her father asked.

"Yes, Daddy," she said. "This is Bobby Blaine. He plays for the San Francisco Giants."

Mr. Moreland looked carefully at Bobby. "You're Bobby Blaine?" he asked.

"Yes, sir."

"I've read about you. They say you're quite a ballplayer."

Bobby laughed. "If you saw the game tonight you might not think so."

Now everyone laughed. They chatted a few more minutes, then Mr. Moreland went back to the desk. When he returned he didn't look happy.

"No room. They claim they're full up. It looks like we're gonna have to find another hotel at this ungodly hour."

"Maybe I can help," Bobby said. "Wait here."

Bobby walked into the bar. He spoke to Manager Hardnet for a few minutes, then returned to the Morelands.

"The team always reserves a couple of extra rooms in case the general manager or one of the owners flies in. My manager says you're welcome to one of them."

In a few minutes, everything was set. Mr. and Mrs. Moreland thanked Bobby and Gus Hardnet. Then Mrs. Moreland said they had had a long day and needed some sleep.

"So do I," Bobby said. "We've got an afternoon game tomorrow."

But before he left, he asked Janet if she would still be there the next night. She said yes, and he offered to take her to dinner and maybe a movie. Her father nodded.

Bobby returned to his room. He lay down and began to drift off. For the first time in months he wasn't thinking about baseball. Instead, he was looking forward to seeing Janet Moreland again. And for the first time in months he felt just 17 years old. That was a good feeling.

17

Bobby had asked the Morelands if they wanted to come to the ballgame. But they had decided to see some of the historical sites around the city and didn't want to change their plans. As he warmed up, he kind of wished Janet could be there.

His parents had called in the morning. They had heard about his error the night before and wanted to see if he was all right. He told them about his mood before he met Janet. They seemed worried. He tried to assure them that he was fine.

But he really wasn't sure. When he trotted out to centerfield for the bottom of the first inning, he felt strangely nervous. It was a different kind of nervous than his first game. That was simply butterflies, the good kind of nervous. The kind that gets a ballplayer pumped up. As Bobby watched Bob Williams deliver the first pitch of the ballgame, he realized what it was.

He was scared.

It was a new feeling for Bobby Blaine. And with two outs in the inning, the Phillies' batter lofted a fly ball to Bobby's right. He drifted over, tapped his glove, and made the catch. But he felt the ball slip a bit as it hit his glove. That didn't help.

Willie Stockton must have noticed, because when Bobby looked over at him, Willie said, "Take it easy, kid."

Bobby's first at bat in the second inning wasn't any better. He was badly fooled on a change-up and fanned. As he returned to the outfield, he knew what was happening but didn't know what to do about it. He was getting psyched out.

In the fifth inning, with the Giants leading 2-1, Bobby fielded a base hit and threw behind the runner, allowing him to take an extra base. It led to the tying run when the next batter hit a sacrifice fly to right. In the dugout, Manager Hardnet came up to him.

"What's the matter, kid? You're a little shaky out there."

"I'm all right," Bobby said.

"Don't con me," the manager said. "There's too much at stake for anyone to play hero."

With two men on in the seventh, Bobby popped up on a curve to kill the rally. And when he went to grab his glove to take the field, he felt Manager Hardnet's hand on his shoulder.

"I'm sending Tolbert out there for you. Maybe you need a rest."

Bobby sat down at the end of the bench. He was glad Janet Moreland hadn't come. Philadelphia won the game, 5-2, and the mood in the clubhouse was very down. It didn't help when Hardnet told

Bobby that Tolbert would be starting the Sunday game.

"I think you need a couple of days to get it together again," he said. "Maybe there's been too much pressure. It's been a tough few weeks."

Bobby was getting dressed when Jeff Cooper walked past him.

"Looks like the honeymoon's over, hotshot," Cooper said.

Suddenly Bobby snapped. He grabbed Jeff and slammed him into the lockers, pinning him there with a viselike grip on his uniform shirt.

"I'm telling you one last time," Bobby shouted. "Lay off me!"

Cooper looked scared as Stockton, Ray Marlin, and Manager Hardnet pulled Bobby off. The manager chewed out both players and said the next time it happened, heads would roll. Bobby dressed quickly and left the clubhouse. The pressure of a championship pennant race seemed to be getting to everyone, especially after two tough losses.

Bobby took Janet to dinner at a small restaurant around the corner from the hotel. But he wasn't very good company. He kept thinking about being pulled from the ballgame. That had never happened to him before. Never.

"You're not even eating," Janet said. "Is it something I said?"

"Oh, no," said Bobby. "It's me. I had a lousy game today, that's all. Guess I'm not used to it."

"I still can't believe you're a big league ball-player," Janet said, sipping her Coke. "You remind me a little of a boy I know back home. But he's just a kid."

Bobby looked up. "What makes me any different?" he asked. "All the guys on the team call me kid."

"I didn't mean anything. It's just that, well, you hang out with grown men."

"I don't hang out with them," he said. "They're just my teammates. I used to play in a men's league back home, but after the game I always went out with my friends."

"I guess it's just that I can't imagine you being a professional athlete. You've even got another year of high school. What are you going to do about that?"

"The team may want me to play winter ball. A lot of young players do that. They promised to get me tutors so I'd finish school and graduate."

"What about your friends? What about the other things that go with being a senior? Class day? The prom? The fun of graduation?"

Bobby really hadn't thought about these things, or about missing them. Baseball always had been number one with him. And it always had been fun. But part of the fun was hanging out with Josh and his other friends after the game. It sure wasn't the same with the Giants.

After dinner, the two walked slowly back to the

hotel, where they sat in the lobby and talked for nearly two hours. Bobby was relaxed. He liked Janet a lot and knew he would miss her when she left the next day.

"Do you think we'll ever see each other again?" he asked.

Janet laughed. "Well, I can always see you on television."

"Very funny."

"It's true."

"Hey, that's not fair. You can see me but I can't see you."

"Well, we might have to do something about that. Doesn't Boston have a team?"

"They're in the other league. We don't play them."

"All right. I'll make you a deal. If you finish high school in Caldwell, I'll come to your senior prom . . . that is, if you want me to."

Bobby laughed. "I just may hold you to that."

The two talked some more. Bobby walked Janet to her room. Then he leaned forward and kissed her. She smiled and kissed him back.

"The prom, eh?" he said.

"If I can wait that long."

They touched hands once more, then Janet went inside.

Bobby took a deep breath and walked slowly back to his room. "At least something good has come of all this," he thought, "now if I can only solve my baseball problems."

When he entered the room, there was a message waiting for him. It was a telegram. He opened it.

"Arriving Philly tomorrow," it read. "See you after the game."

And it was signed, "Barney Rogers."

18

Bobby didn't start the game the next day. Sitting on the bench, he still had plenty to think about. He watched Ricky Tolbert back in centerfield. And he found himself hoping Tolbert would do well. After another minute, he realized why. If Tolbert played well, he, Bobby, probably wouldn't get in the game. It was the first time in his life he ever remembered *not* wanting to play baseball.

Then he thought about Barney. It sure would be good seeing the old man again. But what would he say to Barney? "Take me home" seemed a good way to start. Bobby caught himself. Was he really thinking these things? Had playing in the major leagues, his lifelong dream, gone sour that fast?

All of a sudden, he realized it was the fifth inning, and he didn't even know the score. He looked up to see the Giants losing, 4-2. The Phillies were batting, and their big first baseman sent a deep drive into the right centerfield gap. Both Tolbert and Stockton were racing for the ball at top speed.

Bobby jumped up. He saw the angle and the

speed at which they were pursuing the ball. The. he knew. The two outfielders were going to collide!

The collison was one of the worst in years. Both men lay motionless on the outfield grass as the trainer, manager, coaches, and players all raced out to them. It didn't look good.

In a few seconds, Ricky Tolbert began coming around. He was dizzy and said his head hurt. Probably a concussion, the trainer said. They led Tolbert slowly off the field as the fans gave him a hand. But Stockton was another story. For the veteran, they needed a stretcher.

It was his left knee. The pain was intense. And the worried look on the trainer's face told Bobby the injury was a bad one. As they carried the right-fielder off, Bobby heard the trainer say:

"I think he blew out the knee. Better call the hospital and get Dr. Fargus ready. He's probably gonna have to operate."

Stockton was conscious now, his face twisted in pain as they carried him into the dugout. Bobby leaned over and touched the veteran on the shoulder.

"You'll be all right, Willie," he said. "I know you will."

Stockton looked up. "I'm done, kid. It's over."

Then they carried him down the runway to the clubhouse. Bobby was about to sit down again when he heard Manager Hardnet growl, "Blaine. This ain't no country club. Get out there."

Bobby grabbed his glove and trotted out to centerfield. But all he could think about was Willie Stockton's knee. He had never seen a collision like that, or for that matter, such a bad injury. He just couldn't get his mind on the ballgame, and two batters later it showed when he misplayed an easy fly ball and the Phillies got a double.

The rest of the game was a disaster. Not only were the Giants blown out, 12-4, but Bobby struck out in his only two at bats, made another error, and stopped cold in left center when he heard the leftfielder coming toward him. All he could think about was that collision.

When the game ended, Bobby just slumped on the bench in the dugout. Even after the other players had gone to the clubhouse, he still sat there. Alone. Then there was someone standing beside him, a hand on his shoulder. He looked up. It was Barney.

"I'm not used to being in dugouts," the old man kidded.

"I'm beginning to wish I wasn't," Bobby answered. "But it's good to see you. Where are you coming from?"

"Idaho. Might have found a good left-hander out there. In fact, I'll be heading back tomorrow."

"Then why did you fly all the way to Philly?"

"To see you."

"Just to see me?"

"Do I need an excuse?"

"Maybe."

"Yeah, well, they kind of thought I might find out what's bothering you."

Now Bobby understood. Someone had sent for Barney, and he was just following orders. In a way, it made Bobby angry, but he still was glad to see his old friend.

"Guess I'm just in a little slump, that's all," Bobby said. "I'll snap out of it."

"I don't think you will," Barney confided.

Bobby was surprised by his friend's answer. After all, he was the man who had talked Bobby into going with the Giants. Now he was acting as if there were something really wrong.

"Have you ever been in a slump before, Bobby?" he asked. "Ever in your life?"

"Well, no. Not really."

"You homesick lately?" Barney asked.

"A little, but what's wrong with that? I've never been away from home before."

"Yeah, but I bet that didn't happen until the so-called slump. Right?"

Bobby thought a minute. Barney was right. In fact, he had hit the nail on the head.

"How did you know?" he found himself wondering.

"I knew another kid who went through the same thing a long time ago," the old man said. "It's something that can happen to very young ballplayers."

"What can happen?"

"You're from a small town and you've always

been a star, haven't you? Or to be more specific, *the* star. Right?"

"I guess so," Bobby nodded, still not sure what his friend meant.

"Tell me this," Barney continued. "Have you ever really failed in a big game back home, struck out with the bases loaded, or dropped a fly with the game on the line?"

"No."

"And did anyone ever criticize you in Caldwell?"

"No."

"Did your teammates ever get down on you, blame you for losing a game back there?"

"No."

"But it all happened here, didn't it? And all since your mysterious slump."

Bobby took a deep breath. "How did you know?" he asked.

"Like I said, I once knew a kid it happened to, a small-town kid who didn't know what it was like to fail. He had always been the star, the hero, the guy most admired by his friends. That kid had to learn how to fail. Everybody does. And it's a tough lesson, believe me. Some guys can't learn it in the majors, and it turns their big league dream into a nightmare."

Bobby looked at the old black man, who smiled at him and again touched him on the shoulder.

"Who was the other kid it happened to?" Bobby asked.

"Kid named Barney Rogers who thought he had the world at his feet. When Jackie Robinson broke the color line in 1947 and black players finally got into the majors, I thought I was going to be the biggest star that ever came down the pike. The Giants signed me at 17 and up I came." Barney laughed. "And two months later, down I went. It took another two years before I was really ready."

Bobby couldn't believe Barney was telling him this. "What do we do?" he finally asked. "Am I going to the minors?"

"Probably not now, especially with Stockton out. But Gus will probably spot you the rest of the year, some starts, some pinch-hitting. But you've got to realize you can't be the star every game. Babe Ruth wasn't. Willie Mays wasn't. Reggie wasn't. Not Mattingly or Strawberry. None of them."

"I know," Bobby said.

"Bobby Blaine the person might know, but Bobby Blaine the ballplayer still has to learn," Barney said. "It may take a little more time, but I have a hunch it will all work out."

"Like it did for Barney Rogers?"

"Even better. Barney Rogers didn't have your natural talent. Take it from a wise old scout."

19

WELCOME HOME, BOBBY!

The big sign was stretched across Main Street on the road leading into town. Bobby grinned when he saw it. It was so good to be back in Caldwell.

After they had been swept by the Phils, the Giants had gone into a bad slump. By September 1, they were 11 games out of first place and fading fast. The team just wasn't good enough to win the pennant yet. They still needed more good players. But they were getting closer.

Bobby never really got out of his slump. He only played in spots until the first week in September. Then, after a meeting with Gus Hardnet, Barney Rogers, and his parents, it was decided he should go home. That way, he could start his senior year at Caldwell High with his classmates. And right after graduation, he would join the Giants' rookie league and start all over again. Most people figured he had a good chance of being back in the majors before the next year was out.

"We're all very proud of you, Bobby," his father said after a celebration at the Caldwell Town Hall.

"And we're gonna have one heck of a party at home tonight. Everyone's invited."

Bobby nodded. He was being treated like a hero once again. In a way it felt good. But this time it was different. He knew he wasn't the same person who had gone off to pursue a dream just three months earlier. He had learned a great deal, and he only hoped the lessons would stay with him when he went away the next time.

"You've got to tell me all about it," Josh said as soon as they had time to talk. "I want to know everything. What's Willie Stockton really like, and Jackie Ross? You must have had a ball. I don't know why you even came home."

"Maybe I missed you guys," Bobby said, "and sodas at Boswell's, fishing down by Cramer's Creek, hitting stones in my backyard, and my mother's apple pie."

"You gotta be nuts if you expect me to believe that," Josh said with a wink. "If I were playing for the Giants, you never would have seen me in Caldwell again."

After the party that night, Bobby went to his room. He was dead tired, but it was a good tired. He knew now that he had done the right thing. He would continue to go after his dream. And he also knew he would make it. Baseball was still what he wanted more than anything. But at age 17, he surely could wait another nine months for it all to happen.

Before going to sleep, he had one more thing to do. He had to write a letter to Cambridge, Massachusetts. After all, there was a girl there who had promised to go to the senior prom with him. And he wanted to make sure she didn't forget.

Exercises

Chapter 1

Vocabulary

anxious	instant	obviously
roughed	scout	spotty
tufts	upright	

Exercises

1. What is the main idea of this chapter?
   ___ a. Baseball scout Barney Rogers gives a helpful kid a dollar.
   ___ b. Baseball scout Barney Rogers discovers Bobby Blaine.
   ___ c. Bobby is just under six feet tall.
   ___ d. Barney takes note as he watches Bobby play.

2. When Barney says, "This kid has it all," he means:
   a. Bobby has all the baseballs in town.
   b. Bobby is skilled in all parts of the game.
   c. Bobby is rich, smart, and good-looking.

3. Circle the word that makes the sentence correct.

   The pitcher was a _____ right-hander.
   burlesque   pearly   burly

4. True or False (T or F).
   ___ Barney Rogers stopped in Caldwell, Iowa to look for ball players?

Chapter 2

Vocabulary

barely	bleachers	contract
defending	grinning	quipped
repairs	toast	wit

Exercises

1. What is the main idea of this chapter?
   - ___ a. Bobby and his friends drink soda together.
   - ___ b. Barney Rogers leaves town.
   - ___ c. Bobby wonders whether he'll ever play in the big leagues.
   - ___ d. Bobby's friend, Josh, says he may write to the big league teams and tell them about Bobby.

2. <u>Draw a Line</u>: Connect the definition on the left to the word from the chapter on the right.
   - a. going in   solved
   - b. figured out   wonder
   - c. sticking up for   quipped
   - d. teased   defending
   - e. amazement   entering

3. Why does Barney tell Coach Tuttle not to mention anything to Bobby?

Activity

Bobby's dream is to play for the major leagues. Write a paragraph about a job you really like or dream about. Why do you like it? Explain.

Chapter 3

Vocabulary

beaten path	belt	generation
hotbed	organization	professional
rivalry	rugged	stack up

Exercises

1. What happens after Bobby's game against Dewersville?

2. Underline the *effect* portion of the following statement:

   Bobby's heart pounds with excitement when Barney tells him, "you stack up with the best of them."

3. Which of the words does not describe Barney Rogers?

   ___ a. experienced
   ___ b. leathery
   ___ c. mean
   ___ d. wrinkled

Activity

Imagine you are Bobby and you've just been told you can play in the major leagues. Write a letter to your uncle in San Francisco telling him the unbelievable news. Describe what Barney said and how you felt.

Chapter 4

Vocabulary

contract	cruel	impossible
matter-of-factly	mistake	record
repeated	squarely	success

Exercises

1. What is the main idea of this chapter?
   ___ a. Bobby has never been away from home before.
   ___ b. Bobby arrives home close to dinner time.
   ___ c. Bobby tells his parents that he's going to play in the big leagues.
   ___ d. Mrs. Blaine is the calm one in the house.

2. Underline the *cause* portion of the following statement:

   Mr. and Mrs. Blaine decide there must be some mistake after they hear Bobby's news about his playing baseball for a major league team.

3. Bobby's father thinks that Bobby "broke another record." What does this term mean?

Activity

Write a short story about someone who has important news. Tell who is there and how the people they tell react to it.

Chapter 5

Vocabulary

ability	concerned	conditions
guaranteed	pledged	pressure
prospect	resume	tutors

Exercises

1. Why isn't Barney going to try Bobby in the minor leagues first, before putting him in the big leagues?

2. <u>True or False</u> (Mark T or F):
   - ___ a. Barney wants Bobby to be a second baseman for the Giants.
   - ___ b. Bobby shows Barney a bat that he's had since he was eight.
   - ___ c. The new owners of the Giants want to build a winning team.
   - ___ d. The Giants would make sure Bobby finished school.

3. What does Barney mean when he says that Bobby has "the real goods"?

Activity

Look up Jackie Robinson in an encyclopedia or in another reference book. On a notecard, write down two facts about his life or career that really interest you and explain why. Share the information with your classmates.

Chapter 6

Vocabulary

affecting	division	hovering
pickup	seasoned	shotgun
teasing	uneasy	veteran

Exercises

1. List three reasons why Bobby is worried about going to play for the Giants.

   _____

   _____

   _____

2. <u>Fill in the Blank</u>: Briefly explain what the following sentences mean.

   Manager Hardnet ran a tight ship.

   _____

   Josh couldn't put himself in Bobby's shoes.

   _____

3. How much money will Bobby have made from playing one season of baseball?

   _____

Activity

Imagine you are 17 years old and you're going to earn a lot of money. List five things you would do with the money.

Chapter 7

Vocabulary

ability	blame	broadly
current	gear	legendary
pang	process	roster

Exercises

1. Where do Bobby and Barney drive after they arrive at the airport in San Francisco?

2. Match each of the following people with their corresponding description:

   Mr. Blaine   Carol Pendergast

   Barney Rogers   Doc Hardy

   ___ a. in Bobby's thoughts on the way to the ballpark.

   ___ b. the Giants' equipment manager.

   ___ c. wanted to go on the plane with Bobby but didn't.

   ___ d. took the plane with Bobby.

3. <u>Sequence</u> (number the events in the order in which they happened. 1–4):

   ___ a. Bobby tries on his uniform.

   ___ b. Bobby is a little homesick.

   ___ c. Bobby says goodbye to his mother.

   ___ d. Bobby feels like he can hit .400.

Activity

Bobby flew from Des Moines, Iowa, to San Francisco, California. Look on a map or globe and name the states he flew over if the plane took the most direct route.

Chapter 8

Vocabulary

adjust   anxious   gruffly

license   neither   pot belly

skipper   slight   utility

Exercises

1. Who are the main characters in this chapter?
    - ___ a. Bobby, Barney, and Dugan
    - ___ b. Jeff Cooper and Barney
    - ___ c. Dugan, Jeff Cooper, and Bobby
    - ___ d. Bobby, Manager Hardnet, and Jeff Cooper

2. Manager Hardnet asks his players to give 100 percent, to not make mistakes, and to:
    - ___ a. have team spirit.
    - ___ b. win.
    - ___ c. outsmart the other team.
    - ___ d. look calm while playing.

3. <u>Before or After</u> (Circle one):

    Does Bobby meet his roommate before or after he meets manager Hardnet?

Activity

On a piece of paper, write two headings: "Small Town" and "City". Then list at least 3 advantages and 3 disadvantages of living in each place.

Chapter 9

Vocabulary

arrived	blame	cramp
disgust	hardly	hotshot
intend	sober	whirled

Exercises

1. List three reasons why it's such a change for Bobby to be living with Jeff.

2. <u>Draw a Line</u>: Connect the definition on the left to the word on the right.

   a. not drunk   whirled

   b. strong dislike   sipping

   c. drinking   sober

   d. turned quickly   disgust

3. <u>Fact or Opinion</u> (Mark F or O):

   _____a. Jeff shook his head and kept driving.

   _____b. Billy Dugan was a good friend.

   _____c. Jeff was reading a book.

Activity

Jeff and Bobby got off to a bad start as roommates. List 2 things each of them could have done differently to avoid problems between them.

Chapter 10

Vocabulary

advice	attract	chirped
entire	finest	flinch
gimmick	glaring	hustle

Exercises

1. What is the main idea of this chapter?
   - ___ a. Bobby proves he is a great baseball player.
   - ___ b. Stockton is coming to the end of a fine career.
   - ___ c. Barney isn't at Bobby's first practice.
   - ___ d. After the team finishes practicing, Bobby works out some more on his own.

2. <u>Cause and Effect</u>: What are three things that might have happened when Bobby started getting hits? Write them below.

   _____

   _____

   _____

3. Do you think Bobby is nervous or calm during his first practice? What clues does the chapter give?

   _____

   _____

Activity

Imagine you are a reporter doing a story on Bobby's first practice with the Giants. List five questions you would ask Bobby.

Chapter 11

Vocabulary

ace	bottom	fling
practice	series	spent
victory		

Exercises

1. What is the main idea of this chapter?

2. <u>Draw a Line</u>: Connect the name on the left to the job on the right.
   a. Tom Ramsey   batting coach
   b. Irv Randall   catcher
   c. Ray Marlin   pitcher
   d. Roger Sarason   third baseman

3. <u>Fill in the Blank:</u> Circle the word that makes each sentence correct. Write that word in the blank.
   a. Bobby could feel a _____ run up his spine.
      child   chill   drill
   b. The Braves hung on for the _____.
      victory   victrola   viceroy
   c. Bobby grabbed his bat from the _____.
      track   back   rack
   d. Ray Marlin _____.
      signed   fumbled   singled

Activity

Imagine the Giants-Braves game is over and you are one of the following people. Describe your thoughts and feelings about the game.

Bobby	Tom Ramsey
Irv Randall	Ricky Tolbert

Chapter 12

Vocabulary

ability	affect	apologize
calculate	drifting	guilt
sensed	situations	touchy

Exercises

1. Why do you think Bobby stays on the phone so long?

2. <u>Cause and Effect</u>: Underline the *cause* portion of the following statement.

   After talking to Josh, Bobby worried about whether playing baseball would become just a job.

3. What does Josh mean when he says, "Don't lay a guilt trip on me because I can't run over to Chicago or St. Louis to watch you play."

Activity

Hardnet talks about his team being in a pennant race, which, in baseball, means playing in the championship. Check an almanac and write down, by year, the teams that have won the World Series since 1975. Note whether any team won more than once during that period.

Chapter 13

Vocabulary

glanced	impact	lunged
ovation	pressure cooker	retreated
scampered	souvenir	trotted

Exercises

1. What is the main idea of this chapter?
   ___ a. Baseball becomes fun again for Bobby, as he helps his team win a game.
   ___ b. Tolbert talks to Bobby before the game.
   ___ c. The crowd cheers for Bobby.
   ___ d. Bobby's teammates throw him in the shower.

2. Bobby's roommate could have given him a ride to the ballpark, but Bobby chose to take a cab. Why?

3. <u>Fact or Opinion</u> (Mark F or O):
   _____ The Giants went on to win the game.
   _____ Just a few weeks ago, I was playing for a small high school in Iowa.
   _____ You're a pretty cool dude.

Activity

Imagine you have to write a brief article on the Giants-Braves game. Describe what happened, using your own words.

Chapter 14

Vocabulary

crucial   destiny   front-running
fuss   management   relations
social   stake   uneasy

Exercises

1. What would be a good title for this chapter?

2. <u>Which is Which</u>? Match each of the following
    places with a description below.

    Philadelphia   Iowa   Bay Area

    San Francisco   Hollywood

    a._____   home of the Giants
    b._____   city where the Giants play next
    c._____   reporters came from this region
    d._____   city famous for making movies
    e._____   Bobby's parents flew back here

3. Why does Bobby feel uncomfortable when the
    reporters ask him about his social life?

Activity

In the library, ask for a book with a story of David
and Goliath. Write a brief paragraph explaining
how Bobby is, or is not, like David.

Chapter 15

Vocabulary

athletic	chatter	criticizing
drifted	finger pointing	knock off
lobby	remind	sacrifice

Exercises

1. How does Bobby play in the first game in Philadelphia?

2. <u>True or False</u> (Mark T or F):
   ___ a. Hardnet told Bobby, "Hey, it's all right, man."
   ___ b. Bobby talked a lot when he got to the locker room.
   ___ c. Bobby felt he let everyone down.

3. Circle the word that makes each sentence correct.
   a. Tommy fielded the _____.
      bunting   brunt   bunt
   b. Some _____ could finally be heard.
      chatter   chanters   chapters
   c. This club has _____ back all year.
      pounced   bounced   announced

Activity

Choose an activity, other than baseball, and describe how being under pressure can seriously affect a person's performance.

Chapter 16

Vocabulary

deserting   exactly   perked

puzzled   realized   relatives

reserves   ungodly hour

Exercises

1. What is the main idea of this chapter?
   - ___ a. Bobby calls Josh and his parents.
   - ___ b. Bobby meets a girl and cheers up.
   - ___ c. Bobby thinks about his mistakes.
   - ___ d. Tolbert has friends in Philadelphia.

2. <u>Cause and Effect</u>: Underline the *cause* and *effect* portions of the following statement.

   They claim that they're full. It looks like we're gonna have to find another hotel.

3. Why do you think Janet was unsure about talking to Bobby?

Activity

Mr. and Mrs. Moreland want to show Janet and Jimmy the city. Look up Philadelphia in an encyclopedia, almanac, or guidebook. List four places that the Morelands might visit.

Chapter 17

Vocabulary

assure   chewed out   deliver
lousy   psyched out   pumped up
sites   viselike

Exercises

1. Where do Bobby and Janet agree to meet again?

   _____

2. <u>Sequence</u> (Number the events in the order in which they happened. 1-4):

   ___ a. Bobby has a fight with a teammate.
   ___ b. Bobby gets a telegram.
   ___ c. Bobby is pulled from the ballgame.
   ___ d. Bobby and Janet go to dinner.

3. What does Jeff mean when he tells Bobby, "Looks like the honeymoon's over."

   _____

   _____

Activity

List two ways this story could end. Choose one and explain why you think the story might end this way.

Chapter 18

Vocabulary

collision	concussion	confided
conscious	operate	pursuing
slump	specific	stretcher

Exercises

1. Why does Barney fly out to see Bobby?

   _____

   _____

2. <u>Before or After</u> (Circle one):

   Bobby plays in the game before or after the two
   Giants' players collide.

3. Bobby thinks Barney "hit the nail on the head."
   Briefly explain what Bobby means by this.

   _____

   _____

Activity

Look in an almanac or other reference book, and
find a list of all the National League and American
League baseball teams. Write down three team
names for each league and the city that each team
represents.

Chapter 19

Vocabulary

celebration	dead tired	fading
figured	senior	

Exercises

1. What is the main idea of this chapter?
   - ___ a. Josh wants Bobby to tell him all about the Giants.
   - ___ b. Everyone is invited to Bobby's party.
   - ___ c. Bobby is back home and knows he'll make it as a ballplayer.
   - ___ d. Bobby writes a letter to Janet.
2. The party for Bobby is at:
   - ___ a. The Giants' clubhouse.
   - ___ b. Bobby's house.
   - ___ c. Cramer's Creek.
   - ___ d. Boswell's Drugstore.
3. How is Bobby going to make it back into the major leagues again?

Activity

Did the story end the way you thought it would? In a few paragraphs, write a different ending to the story.

About the author

Bill Gutman is a freelance writer who has written some 70 books, many of them for children.

His books include biographies and profiles of many professional athletes, both past and present; a book of short sports stories; and several juvenile novels.

Bill lives in Poughquag, New York, with his wife, two stepchildren, and a lively assortment of pets.

Turman Publishing's Fiction Paperback Series

Smitty

Mark looked at her. He didn't fully understand this pretty girl or what drove her. She was as intense a player as he'd ever seen. Maybe it wasn't such a good idea to take her out on a date, after all. But he'd find out Saturday night. He knew one thing, though. She was one amazing basketball player.

Rookie Summer

Bobby really hadn't thought about these things, or about missing them. Baseball always had been number one with him. And it always had been fun. But part of the fun was hanging out with Josh and his other friends after the game. It sure wasn't the same with the Giants.

The Winner

For a moment, as Bart looked at the Bloomsday brochure, he forgot about the accident. The old dreams came back and he felt a surge of excitement as he thought of actually running in Bloomsday.

Then he saw a photo of a girl in a wheelchair, and he remembered. His hand started to shake and he laid the pamphlet on his bed. He looked at Mr. Peters. Was this some kind of joke?